SPOZ'S SHORTS
AND THE OCCASIONAL
LONG ONE

BY
GIOVANNI
'SPOZ'
ESPOSITO

Illustrations by
Joseph Witchall

First published in Great Britain in 2017
by Caboodle Books Ltd
Copyright © Giovanni Esposito 2017

All rights reserved. Apart from any use permitted under UK
copyright law, this publication may only be reproduced,
stored or transmitted, in any form, or by any means with
prior permission in writing from the publishers or in the case
of reprographic production in accordance with the terms
of licences issued by the Copyright Licensing Agency
and may not be otherwise circulated in any form
of binding or cover other
than that in which it is published and without a
similar condition being imposed on
the subsequent purchaser.

A Catalogue record for this book is available
from the British Library.

ISBN 978-0-9954885-7-1

Illustrations by Joseph Witchall
Page Layout by Highlight Type Bureau Ltd
Printed and bound by CPI Group (UK) Ltd, Croydon, CR0 4YY

The paper and board used in the paperback by
Caboodle Books Ltd are natural recyclable products
made from wood grown in sustainable forests.
The manufacturing processes conform to the environmental
regulations of the country of origin.

Caboodle Books Ltd
Riversdale, 8 Rivock Avenue, Steeton, BD20 6SA
www.authorsabroad.com

Acknowledgements

Some of the poems in this book have popped up in an assortment of other places, before appearing on these pages. It's tough keeping track, and frankly, I haven't done a great job of keeping track, so don't be surprised if you see them popping up in an assortment of other places.

Having said that, I do know that *Even Superheroes Need the Toilet, Eat My Goal, Grandma's Jumper* and *Come With Me* were commissioned by the brilliant 'Poetry On Loan' and have popped up on their marvellous postcards in libraries around the country. I also know that *The Castle Up the Beacon* was commissioned by the BBC for National Poetry Day 2016. Thank you BBC!

I've also lost count of the numbers of websites (as well as which ones) that have displayed some of these poems within their virtual pages. Thank you ... all of you.

To all the schools, school teachers and young people I've worked with and continue to work with ... thank you.

Thank you to the lovely people at Caboodle Books for publishing this, my second poetry book for the young ... and young at heart.

More 'thank yous' in the 'thank you' page at the back. Thank you.

For Claudia,
Francesca
and Zack.

Contents

Hull & Peckham 7

Brum & Belfast 8

King's Cross & King's Heath 9

Even Superheroes Need the Toilet 11

Sophie's Voice 12

Wales & Birmingham City 14

Villa & Fred 15

Binocular Boy 17

Grandma's Jumper 21

Smethwick Town & West Brom 23

Brazil & Bude 24

Stoat 25

Stoke & Football Shirt 26

The Three Legged Fox 27

Carlisle & Gold and Black 32

Max & Hong Kong 33

Abdullah and Lady Ga-Ga 34

Leicester & Dorking 35

Eat My Goal 36

Jack & Jeeves 38

Cairo and Madrid 39

Harvey the Hipster Hamster 41

Bird in a Cage & Greyhound 45

France & Dave 46

Singing & Stressed 47

Come with Me 48

The Poetree 49

Princess Brian & Will 50

Jamaica 51

Bad Diet 52

Elvis McGonigall's Tartan Pants 55

Ferret & Beth 56

Clive & Mouse 57

Black Widow Spider & Deacons 58

Alien 59

Castle Up the Beacon 60

Trump & Geoff 62

The Shire & Surrey 63

Amerah 64

Janet & Merlin 65

I'm a Happy Pirate 66

Benny the Badger Avenger 69

Devon & Ed 73

Milan & Zack 74

Frankie & Claude 75

Angela's Lashes 77

Planet Earth 80

The Alpaca in the Christmas Cracker 82

Thatcher & John Cena 84

Llama & Stephen Fry 85

Kamil & Richards from Limerick 86

Barry's Big Brown Magic Conkers 87

Peckham

There was a young lady from Peckham,
Who looked like Victoria Beckham,
She wasn't that posh,
'Cause she had a moustache,
And if folks dared to point, then she'd deck 'em!

Hull

There was an old lady from Hull,
Who had flowers growing out of her skull,
She picked them each day,
And then gave them away,
'Till the neighbourhood's vases were full.

Brum

There was a young lady from Brum,
Who ate lots of Pedigree Chum,
One night in the dark,
She let out a bark,
And a dog started sniffing her bum!

Belfast

There was a young man from Belfast,
Whose boyish good looks wouldn't last,
He had a face lift,
But got terribly miffed,
When his head ended up in a cast!

King's Cross

A young man called Matt, from King's Cross,
Had hair that looked like candy floss,
He got lots of work,
Painting doors in Dunkirk,
'Cause the French liked the price of his gloss.

King's Heath

There was an old man from King's Heath,
Who had quite remarkable teeth,
When asked "What's your name?"
He replied without shame,
"All of my friends call me Keith".

Even Superheroes Need the Toilet

In any superhero story,
When lives or the world is at stake,
Does that hero or heroine ever utter the phrase,
"Can we pause for a 'comfort' break?"
Because everybody needs to go sometimes,
Yes, we've all been caught on the hop
And everyone knows that, once you start,
You need to carry on until you stop.
If the X-Men developed a master plan,
There'd be one thing sure to foil it...
And that's if, in the midst of battle,
Wolverine stopped to go to the toilet.
And if Gotham were being held to ransom,
Would Batman, from his blackened cowl,
Say "I'm sorry commissioner Gordon, but,
I sense a movement in my bowel"
So spare a thought for poor Wonder Woman,
Whose super powers seem to enhance her,
You can't cross your legs when the planet's in
    need,
'Cause when nature calls, you have to answer.

Sophie's Voice

Sophie's voice was a whisper,
It barely made a squeak,
She preferred to remain unheard,
So she would rarely, ever speak.
She would listen a lot and absorb a lot,
She was really rather bright,
But when it came to arguments,
She was as silent as the night.
She'd watch as people's voices cracked
And screeched with bare emotion,
She'd frown as vicious words were thrown,
With anger and commotion,
But ... one day, she would change all that,
As her patience wore so thin,
Sophie could hold her tongue no more
And finally ... gave in.

A vile old man on the telly,
Who was spreading lies, hate and fear,
Made Sophie raise her voice so much,
That the whole neighbourhood would hear.

"No ..." she said with a gentle murmur,
"No ..." she said once again,

"No, no, no ..." as her volume rose further,
With a truth much too strong to contain.

"No! No! No! No! No! No! No!" she continued,
Each louder than the one before,
With the thirteenth "NO!" the windows
    shattered
And the T.V. screen smashed to the floor!

Sophie seemed a little shocked at first,
She'd never caused quite such a stir,
Everyone stopped ... and everyone listened ...
And all eyes were focussed on her.
What followed next was her calm explanation,
That untangled the lies from fact,
In a way that made better sense of it all,
In a way that other voices had lacked.
See ... Sophie's voice had a power,
That when faced with hate, fear and lies,
Would rise above the distortion
And would open ears and eyes.

Now ... Sophie speaks in confident tones,
She is listened to far and wide,
Which proves, if you have something good to say,
Don't shrink ...
Don't cower ...
Don't hide.

Wales

There was an old lady from Wales,
Who lived in the North Yorkshire Dales,
She missed the great thrill,
Of living in Rhyl,
So survived on a diet of snails!

Birmingham City

A player from Birmingham City,
Liked dancing with girls who were pretty,
He didn't mind,
When they robbed him blind,
Now he's singing the blues – what a pity!

Villa

An old man who once played for Villa,
Was as cute as a baby chinchilla,
His family were weird,
'Cause his wife wore a beard,
And his children all screeched like Godzilla!

Fred

A lonely old shepherd called Fred,
Thought a sheep was the best thing to wed,
He said "They're so kind
And they really don't mind,
When you ask them to sleep in the shed."

Binocular Boy

In the last few gasps of labour's pain,
A birthing mum pushed again and again.
One more contraction and one final heave
And out popped a baby whose name
    would be Steve.

The mid wife was startled and shrieked with
    surprise,
The baby was born with binocular eyes!
Then, at arms length, she passed it to mum,
Who wished she could send it to whence it had
    come.

When mum took him home, the boy's father was
    shocked,
With eyes such as these, he was sure to be
    mocked,
So they hid him away from those that might pry
And under night's cover, young Stephen would
    cry...

But as Stephen grew, his vision grew keener,
Though this later led to the odd misdemeanour,
Stephen's binocular eyes were much more,
Than all of the experts gave him credit for!

Binocular boy with his 50X zoom,
Can see through your windows and into your room,
He looks through your bodies and into your minds,
Then messes around with the things that he
    finds!

A skill such as Steve's was both scary and rare,
Controlling one's thoughts by the weight of his
    stare!
His parents would pander to his every demand,
For now it was Steve who had the upper hand.

Stephen wants biscuits! Stephen wants cake!
One glare from his eyes, they'd be starting to
    bake!
And if they should moan or scoff at his whim,
Their outlook on life would turn horribly grim!

Binocular boy's mom and dad became slaves,
He intended to work them right into their graves,
He bore a big grudge for their callous neglect,
When you're brought up like that – hey, what do
    you expect?

Stephen would often have thoughts that were
    bad,
Of how to humiliate his mom and dad,
With practical jokes that were cruel and uncouth,
Binocular boy was an unhappy youth.

One day as young Steve thought that
    he'd got it all,
He took his binocular eyes off the ball,
Forgetting some lessons he'd been taught in class,
Like not lighting matches when you can smell
    gas...

A massive explosion, like that of a bomb!
Blew up young Steve and his dad and his mom!
Some things can't be seen by the keenest of
    sight...
And two wrongs will definitely not make a right.

Grandma's Jumper

It was a lovely jumper, Grandma,
Just like the kind that I like to wear,
A chunky knit, that's a baggy fit,
The kind that makes passers – by stare.
It may have been the lobster you'd sewn on
   the front,
That drew all the smirks and the sneers,
Or the zombie's face you stitched on the back,
That nearly brought children to tears.

I love the way the sleeves were uneven in length,
At first, I didn't quite understand
Why the left one was shorter than the right one...
Simple really ...it was easier to hold your hand.

You'd wisely dropped stitches all over the place,
Mother said you were losing the plot,
But I knew that those holes had been put there
   on purpose,
To make sure that I didn't get too hot.

I refused to believe that your marbles were lost,
I *knew* you were brilliant and clever,
I just wish you'd have found a knitting pattern,
  Grandma,
That would have knitted your life back together.

Smethwick Town

A lady from old Smethwick town,
Only wore socks that were brown,
She said "There's no catch,
I just like them to match
With the vest under my dressing gown."

West Brom

A poor young boy from West Brom,
Forgot the street name he came from,
He felt a lot better,
'Cause in the back of his sweater,
Was the name and address of his mom.

Brazil

There was a young man from Brazil,
Who couldn't keep his eyebrows still,
When they reached a high speed,
They would make his nose bleed,
What a truly remarkable skill!

Bude

An old Cornish lady from Bude,
Went swimming at night in the nude,
She neglected to think,
That a dip in the drink,
Would turn all her bits to fish food!

Stoat

A wild and reckless young stoat,
Had a boxing match with a large goat,
He took a blow to the head
And in an instant, was dead,
So the goat wrote the stoat a short note ...

..which read ...

I hope that I caused you no pain,
And I'm sorry I smashed in your brain,
Our meeting was fated,
But if you're reincarnated,
Do come back and try me again!

Stoke

There was a young singer from Stoke,
Who was an amiable sort of a bloke,
He joined a boy band,
And won fame through the land,
For flashing his bum as a joke!

Football Shirt

My brother's old blue football shirt,
Got crusty when covered with dirt,
He washed it twice yearly,
Which made the cuffs curly,
And the collar so stiff it would hurt!

The Three Legged Fox

He was spotted by "Shell" from his Halesowen
  drive,
That canine curiosity was very much alive!
The legend lived on, midst the trees and the rocks,
That bushy tailed beasty ... the three legged fox!

An unfortunate triped – with legs of just three,
Made toilet time tricky, especially a wee,
Cocking a leg would leave him bereft,
'Cause the fox couldn't balance on the two
  he had left.

Life was quite tough for our foxy old friend,
But he was determined to buck an old trend,
See ... most "damaged" animals with gouged
  eyes or bust hips,
Would curl up their tails and cash in their chips.

Not so for our hero! Our cunning old critter!
Turned his back on the animals that would tease
  and titter,
Pushed himself to his limits and would go
  to great lengths,
To ignore his weaknesses and work on his
  strengths.

He made for the town and changed his eating
    habits,
Food scraps in dustbins, instead of wild rabbits.
Each day was a challenge of one kind or another,
Just putting two legs in front of the other.

Not before long, he was settling in,
He would forage for food, moving from bin to bin,
Some nights were meager, though others quite
    hearty,
As our teatime waste, provided him with a party.

As night time fell he would follow his nose,
Be fleet on his three feet and nimble on his toes,
Even though he had a few fewer than he should,
He would need to be on them in his new
    neighbourhood.

All kinds of creatures came out after dark,
Some from their houses and some from the park,
Some were more feral, some short and some tall,
Though the ones they called "human"
    were the worst of them all.

Our three legged fox had found a new danger,
Some humans were "human", yet others were
    stranger,
"They're not like us animals" our foxy friend
    thought,
"Because some of these humans kill animals for
    sport."

It was then that the fox remembered his history,
To the times when he walked with four legs –
    not just three ...
And that day when a horn's screech, filled him
    with fear,
As he sensed that imminent peril was near.

The air was thick with sickening sounds,
From men on horseback with packs of hounds,
He knew that he had to get underground fast,
Or the next few moments would be his last.

As he made for his den, a dog knocked him off
    track,
Seized him by his leg, the left one at the back!
As the dog bit in harder, the leg sheared at the
    knee!
Our young fox was hurt, but at least he was free.

He hid in his hole till the hunt had moved on,
Looked back for his leg, which now sadly had
gone.
He rested for days, lived off insects and worms
And made sure that his wound wasn't infected
by germs.

When he finally emerged, he was one leg lighter,
He just got on with his life, because he was a
fighter,
He knew that he'd been much luckier than some,
Because he was alive and had overcome.

So there, he still lives, in the town of Halesowen,
Where the scraps from our tables keep that
old fox goin',
One day he'll go out in a blaze of glory,
And that'll be the end of this under dog story!

Dedicated to "Blind" Dave Heeley

Carlisle

There was a young girl from Carlisle,
Who could brighten a day with her smile,
She let out a cough,
Which knocked her head off,
Now, the sun hasn't shone in a while!

Gold and Black

A young lad dressed in gold and black,
Went in search of a Tibetan Yak,
The field he had camped on,
Was in near Wolverhampton,
So it didn't take long to walk back.

Max

A really rich person called Max,
Found it ever so hard to relax,
He got many pains,
From his ill gotten gains,
Of greed and not paying his tax

Hong Kong

There was a young man from Hong Kong,
Who woke, everyday, with a song,
He'd leap from his bed,
With a tune in his head,
And say, "Nothing today can go wrong!"

Abdullah

There was a young man called Abdullah,
Who filled people's hearts with joy and colour,
He was never greedy,
And helped out with the needy,
So everyone's bellies were fuller.

Lady Ga-Ga

A singer called Lady Ga – Ga,
Stuck fireworks onto her bra,
She let out a cough,
Which set them both off,
And now she's an overnight star.

Leicester

There was a young lady from Leicester,
Who found things just didn't interest her,
She often got bored,
Fell asleep and then snored,
Now all of her family detest her.

Dorking

There was a young surgeon from Dorking,
Who couldn't stop his stomach talking,
He said "That's terrific!
My gut's scientific
And my belly sounds like Stephen Hawking!"

Eat My Goal

Nineteen seventy three – I was the knock kneed
   squirt,
In my hand me down shorts and Birmingham City
   shirt,
Lined up on parade in the park for inspection
And praying not to be last in today's big team
   selection.
What I lacked in skill, I made up with heart,
There was nothing like the thrill of taking part.

Once, last week, I nearly took a shot,
I didn't score a goal, but I ran around a lot!
It was always the big lads that got picked first,
So I puffed out my chest, 'till it was near fit to
   burst,
But there was no wool to be pulled over keenest
   of eyes,
And I was last to be picked again –
   no big surprise.

It was the first team to ten ... battle progressed,
I'd kicked the ball twice ... I was really impressed!

We were on nine ... ball whipped in with pace ...
Back of the net ... it went in off my face!
I was hailed the match winner, there were hugs,
    there was kissing,
There was blood on my shirt and two teeth
    missing!
The teeth soon grew and the pain went away ...
I'm so glad I had a go on that memorable day.

Jack

There was a young pirate called Jack,
Who kept golden coins in a sack,
He had a pet duck,
He kept for good luck,
Who would frighten off thieves with a 'quack'!

Jeeves

A very old butler called Jeeves,
Had bogies stuck on his shirt sleeves,
He cared not a thing,
For in the season of spring,
They looked just like blossoming leaves.

Cairo

There was a young Camel from Cairo,
Who got spun around like a gyro,
His writing went wonky,
And he felt like a Donkey,
When his hump got covered in biro.

Madrid

A bold matador from Madrid,
Fought bulls in a ring for a quid,
He got badly cut,
From a horn in his butt,
Now regrets everything that he did!

Harvey the Hipster Hamster

Harvey was a hipster hamster,
He looked pretty cool yet weird,
On account of his very skinny jeans,
His specs and his bushy beard.

His tight t-shirt said 'geek' on the front,
In very large printed letters,
He would often wear a beanie hat
And great big baggy sweaters.

He'd 'schmooze' around the river bank,
With his skinny decaf soya latte,
Harvey was a dedicated vegan,
So it was 'no' to cheese, sausage and pate.

Harvey listened to the coolest bands
That gigged at The River's Edge Bar,
And of all the cool dudes that played there,
Justin Beaver was the coolest by far.

Justin was the singer in 'The Badger's Set',
A band with a hip reputation,
They could curl the whiskers on a weasel's
nose
And bring hedgehogs out of hibernation.

Now ... Harvey got a little bit jealous
Of Justin's adoring attention,
So he began to hatch a horrible plan,
With a nasty and evil intention!

He was aware that Justin loved to swim,
Just like many beavers do,
But there was a peril that lurked in the river's
   reeds,
That only Harvey knew.

Magnus, the pike, was a terrible fish,
He gobbled up ducklings and stoats,
Harvey had even seen him
Attack fishermen in their boats!

If Harvey could lure Justin,
To the edge of the river, by the reeds,
He was sure that he could leave Magnus,
To complete his gruesome deeds ...

So ... one warm night at The River's Edge Bar,
As The Badger's Set finished their show,
Harvey saw Justin wandering off,
Under the moonlight's glow.

"Hey dude!" called Harvey, "You're the coolest
    dude!"
"Thanks dude!" Justin said in reply,
"Can we take a little walk by the river?" asked
    Harvey,
"There're some moorhens who want to say 'hi'".

So off they swaggered by the light of the moon,
Toward the expected end of our story,
Though neither Justin nor Harvey knew
Of the night time menace called ... Tory.

Tory's heart was as cold as stone,
She snapped with a ghastly beak,
When night time came, she liked to prey
On the vulnerable, small and weak.

Tory was a tawny owl,
She had cunning and stealth in gallons,
She silently soared under cover of night,
To grab creatures with her talons!

Now, Tory didn't want to risk getting hurt,
And they say that owls are wise,
Beavers are a little too large and strong,
Where as hamsters are ... just the right size!

Poor old Harvey never stood a chance,
Snatched away in a single swoop,
He was turned into a meal for the awful Tory
And then turned into owl pellets and poop!

So ... if you ever have bad intentions
You want to inflict on someone else,
You'd better think twice ...
And try to be nice ...
It will be better for your health.

Bird in a Cage

A poor pretty bird in a cage,
Was born to perform on the stage,
It came on to some "Arrrrs",
Then squeezed through the bars,
And demanded a fair working wage.

Greyhound

A greyhound that ate lots of cheese,
Had knobbly bits on his knees,
He got into habits,
Of chasing small rabbits
And cocking his leg against trees.

France

There was a young lady from France,
Who loved nothing more than a dance,
She got a big shock,
When she tripped on her frock,
And ended a twirl in her pants.

Dave

A wonderful barber called Dave,
Would charge seven pounds for a shave,
His razor and soap,
Was approved by the Pope,
And a hairy old man from a cave.

Singing

A young man who thought he could sing,
Was given a big diamond ring,
He burst into song,
That went horribly wrong,
So his head was removed by the king.

Stressed

When times are a little bit stressed,
And you're finding it hard to get dressed,
Just say "I can do it",
Then just muddle through it
And you will feel really impressed!

Come With Me ...

Frog's spawn Saturday mornings,
Slightly deaf to our Mothers' warnings,
We'd set our sights on hidden jewels,
Amidst the hills and woods and pools.

Precious jellies, with my best friends,
Would stare up through their fish eye lens,
Just out of reach ... so time to wade
And onwards with our kids' crusade.

Off with shoes and off with socks,
Watch out for those jagged rocks!
Swampy squelches between each toe,
As muddy clouds began to grow.

We'd gaze down at the splendid soup,
We'd fill our jars with a joyful scoop,
Messy and merry in equal measure,
We'd head back home with our tapioca treasure.

"Come with me" you used to say
And I knew we were in for a special day,
Memories grow where the days once grew,
Those blessed blossoms of '72.

The Poetree

There's a tree at the bottom of our garden,
It's not like any other tree,
Instead of leaves and branches,
It's got WORDS in it's canopy.
The rest of the garden isn't so strange,
It grows shrubs and flowers and herbs,
But that strange old tree just isn't the same,
As it grows adjectives and verbs.
Weird things happen to creatures
That land or climb in that tree -
As a cat jumped onto it's trunk,
It changed ... into C – A – T
I saw a sparrow land there once
And instantly I knew,
It would change into S – P – A – R – R
Oh and double you.
And as the wind blows, it's not leaves that fall
On our lawn and flower bed,
It's letters that tumble and float and drop,
Every one from A to Z

Princess Brian

A beautiful princess called Brian,
Had a grip that was stronger than iron,
Her voice was quite gentle,
But if you drove her mental,
She'd let out a roar like a lion!

Will

A magical archer called Will,
Made an arrow from an old writer's quill,
It wrote in the sky,
As it went whizzing by,
Which gave all the poets a thrill!

Jamaica

A caring young man from Jamaica,
Had a knack for being a dream maker,
His mom had the notion,
Of sailing the ocean,
So he promised, one day, that he'd take her.

Now the caring young man was quite clever,
He realised their naval endeavour,
By building a boat,
Out of stuff that would float,
That he bought from a nice man called Trevor.

They set off to sea in their craft,
Though some people thought they were daft,
When they got to St. Kitts,
Their boat was in bits,
But oh! How the family laughed!

Bad Diet

I've been feeling a little bit grubby,
I've been feeling a little bit grotty,
I've been getting a lot of discomfort,
I've had quite a bad jelly botty.

My diet's been all out of balance,
I've been skipping on my fruit and veggies,
I've been walking around in school today,
Like I've been given some serious wedgies.

That chocolate cake I ate the other night,
Washed down with that extra piece,
Came flying out the very next day,
Like a flock of angry geese!

Make sure you drink lots of water,
It's good for your body's hydration,
Gobble high fibre and skip on the fat,
To avoid a dose of constipation.

Treat your tummy with respect,
Don't feed it with stuff that's obscene,
For that junk food will come back and haunt you,
As it makes its way down the latrine.

So say "No!" to that unhealthy burger,
Throw out those sweets if you've got 'em,
'Cause at the end of the day, a bad diet doesn't
   pay,
But it pays to be good to your bottom.

Elvis McGonagall's Tartan Pants

Elvis McGonagall wore his tartan pants
On the outside of his 'troosers',
It made him feel like Superman,
As he battled with bullies and bruisers.
He was nae one for fisticuffs,
For he was a man of words,
His head was a little up in the clouds,
Away with the fairies and birds.
He'd always shout "Revolution!"
From the comfort of his arm chair,
Then snuggle down for forty winks,
In his tartan underwear.
He'd wake with a start, "Revolution!" he'd cry
And onto his feet he would leap,
Then sit back down in his tartan pants
And calmly, nod back off to sleep.
In his dreams he had super powers,
He was the saviour of human kind,
He could fly into burning buildings
And control things with his mind!
But when he woke, life got in the way
Of his heroic, revolutionary roar,
So he wrote a few more poems
And stuck them on Radio Four.

Ferret

A cunningly cute little ferret,
Had a fortune that he might inherit,
His folks said "Look son,
You're not our number one –
It's unlikely that you'll ever get it"

N.B. If you say "get it" in a good Brummie accent,
you can "gerit" to rhyme perfectly with "ferret"
and "inherit". Trust me on this.

Beth

A marvellous Eagle called Beth,
Would frighten small children to death,
But she was always so good ...
Just misunderstood,
On account of her rather bad breath.

Clive

A stunning young drummer called Clive,
Parked a car full of drums on his drive,
The snare did a roll,
That squashed a poor mole
And the cymbals were buried alive!

Mouse

There once was a mouse in a garage,
Who looked a bit like Nigel Farridge,
He wasn't that nice,
'Cause he hated the mice,
Who'd arrived on the back of a carriage.

Black Widow Spider

A menacing black widow spider,
Took to the skies in a glider,
She got rather scared,
'Cause she wasn't prepared,
So she steadied her nerves with some cider.

Deacons

A group of Catholic deacons,
Sought hair do's that stood out like beacons,
They settled on mullets,
For their heads were like bullets,
And they really did not suit Mohicans.

Alien

My mom gave birth to an alien,
Its head was shaped like a cone,
My dad was onto the tabloids,
On the hospital telephone.
It was purple-ish blue, with a crimson hew,
Its flesh was like a shrivelled up prune,
It shrieked like a terrible banshee,
With the face of a scary baboon!
From the second it popped out of mother,
It screeched to be feed with some food,
And the noises that came from its bottom,
Were rotten and rancid and rude.
The midwife didn't know who to slap first,
As the alien flapped like a flounder,
So she turned to my mom and said calmly,
"Mrs Spoz, it's a bonnie ten pounder!"
Mom was so chuffed, as she'd huffed and
    she'd puffed,
She was happy, yet tired and sore,
But this alien wasn't her first one …
It was only the second of four!
So mom and dad, let me say "thank you!",
'Cause the struggle, I know was a daily one,
Yet we smiled in the face of adversity,
And it's been really ace being born an alie – on.

The Castle Up the Beacon

I can see your house from here ...
In fact ... I can see **all** of your houses from here ...
And when the weather's clear
And the sky's as blue as a Saturday afternoon at
   St. Andrew's,
Win or lose, I will always choose ... this.
I'm your borderland beacon that bore down on
   you from birth,
Giving Rubery a view like 'Google Earth'
Before you even knew what computers were.

They call me a 'toposcope' these days,
But I will always be your castle ...
More than just a Cadbury treat sat upon this
   grassy hill,
And from this toppest top it's hard to see
The veins of your rich realities,
Your variety of societies and your diverse
   nationalities.

Zoomed out up here hides the hustle and hurry
   of you,
Webbed feet flapping like the clappers,
When all I see is a swan ... but I know what goes on.

I've felt it in the happy skips of inner city
   children,
I've heard it in the banter of a hundred different
   languages,
I've smelt it in a thousand trades
Of glass and cars and chocolate,
I've sampled it in spices, samosas and cheese
   sandwiches.

I've been watching Birmingham
And The Black Country grow, up here,
I can see roads like rivers, ebb and flow, up here,
I've wept with family generations as they come
   and go, up here,
I've seen the fervent kisses of mistletoe, up here.

I've chuckled at tangled kite strings and clumsy
   gamboles,
Laughed at pet dog picnic pirates as they
   plundered ham roles,
I'm the fortress in the forest that you long to get
   lost in,
I'm the smile on your face …
I am ace,
I am bostin.

Trump

There was a old president called Trump,
Who was brought down to Earth with a bump,
He came to an end,
When Nigel, his friend,
Took all of his wigs to the dump.

Geoff

There was an old badger called Geoff,
Who was training to be a top chef,
The customers yelled,
Poor Geoff was expelled,
And he's also gone partially deaf!

The Shire

There was a big horse from the Shire,
Who liked to join in with the choir,
At the end of the day,
He could only sing "neigh",
Yet he fulfilled his own heart's desire!

Surrey

There was a young lady from Surrey,
Who needed the loo in a hurry,
When asked "What's the cause,
Of the smell in your draws?"
She answered "I think it's the curry".

Amerah

There was a young girl called Amerah,
Who spoke loudly so people could hear her,
Her weapons of choice,
Were her words and her voice,
With a message that could not be more clearer...

"Be good to each other!" she'd say,
"Help each other work, rest and play.
Don't be a div,
Just live and let live,
You'll feel better at the end of the day!"

Janet

There was an old lady called Janet,
Who gobbled up fish like a Gannet,
Her flatulent gasses,
Could steam up your glasses,
Which wasn't too good for the planet!

Merlin

There was an old wizard called Merlin,
Who couldn't stop his beard from curlin',
A German hairdresser,
Said "It will curl lesser,
If you come over and live in Berlin"

I'm a Happy Pirate!

I'm a happy pirate … aaarrrgggghhh!
My beard is long and yellow,
I'm not like other pirates,
Because I'm a friendly fellow!

I'm a happy pirate … aaarrrgggghhh!
I drink milk instead of rum,
It gives me stronger teeth and bones
And pimples on my bum!

I'm a happy pirate … aaarrrgggghhh!
My wooden leg is made to measure,
I land upon uncharted shores,
To look for buried treasure!

I'm a happy pirate … aaarrrgggghhh!
Long John Silver is my mate,
There's a parrot on his shoulder,
That keeps saying "pieces of eight!".

I'm a happy pirate … aaarrrgggghhh!
There's a cutlass at my side,
I don't think I've ever used it,
Because I run away and hide!

I'm a happy pirate … aaarrrggghhh!
My ship's called "Saucy Sally",
There's a "Jolly Rodger" on the mast
And mermaids in the galley!

I'm a happy pirate … aaarrrggghhh!
And I sail the seven seas,
My ship goes fast in a good strong wind,
But slowly in a breeze!

I'm a happy pirate … aaarrrggghhh!
I've got a patch over one eye,
It got pooped on by an Albatross,
When I looked up in the sky!

Benny the Badger Avenger

From St. Ives to Sunderland,
East Fife to Fulham,
Some frightened young farmers,
Were trying to cull 'em!

Those black and white faces,
So cute and so free,
Were being blamed for the spread,
Of bovine TB.

A horrible sickness
That could lay waste to cattle,
So those frightened young farmers,
Got ready for battle.

But the badgers couldn't help it,
It just wasn't fair,
As the plague could have been cured,
With more compassion and care.

All of those nasty,
Unnecessary exterminations,
Could have easily been replaced,
By some simple vaccinations.

So ... out from his set
Stepped a badger called Benny,
Who would fight for all badgers,
Both the few ... and the many!

He helped badger families
Escape hunter's paws,
With his bravery and cunning
And some swipes from his claws!

His friends of the forest
Were so smart and so clever
And they all understood,
They were stronger together.

So when hunters came hunting,
Under cover of night,
Benny called up his forest friends ...
"Animals unite!"

Foxes and badgers,
Rabbits and stoats,
Roebucks and blackbirds,
Buzzards and goats!

All colours of animals,
Some sombre, some vivid,
Were not only wild,
They were positively livid!

They stood up to the hunters
And chased them away,
So the badger population,
Could live another day!

So let's hear it for Benny!
The badger avenger!
Protecting his species,
From malice and danger!

A hero for badgers
And an example to us,
Stand up to the bullies ...
And kick up a fuss!

Devon

There was a guitarist from Devon,
Whose amplifier went up to eleven,
It was loud as a bomb,
It would frighten his mom,
So she made him restrict it to seven.

Ed

There was a cool young man called Ed,
Whose hair was an orangey red,
His guitar skills were neat,
Sang and rapped to a beat,
Which has stood him in really good stead!

Milan

There was a young man from Milan,
Who kept himself cool with a fan,
His mama said "Joe,
If you don't let it go,
You'll blow the moustache from your gran"

Zack

There was a young drummer called Zack,
Who liked to give his drums a whack,
He once did a piddle,
In a long para-diddle,
Now his band members won't have him back!

Frankie

A ginger young lady called Frankie,
Was only a little bit cranky,
She said "Oh how cute,
Look at that parachute,
I may turn it into a hankie!"

Claude

There was a cool mother called Claude,
Who was worshipped and loved and adored,
She was always so kind,
And quite easy to find,
In a cupboard where good things are stored.

Angela's Lashes

Angela's lashes just grew and grew,
Like curtains in front of her eyes,
Way past her cheeks and down past her chest,
Beyond her waist and her thighs.

She would trim them down each night before bed,
Though her efforts were all in vain,
For as soon the sun began a new day,
Her lashes had sprouted again!

Her constant snipping wore her down,
So she embraced them in all their glory,
Lashes like hers were rather unique,
Which leads us into our story ...

A rotten young lad would tease Angela,
About her long and flowing lashes,
He often tried to set them on fire,
In an attempt to reduce them to ashes!

He would laugh and poke fun and often be rude,
Which made poor Angela sad,
So her lashes took it upon them selves,
To get back at the nasty young lad ...

One night in June as Angela slept,
She had a nightmare about the horrible bully
And as she tossed and turned in her tormented
    sleep,
Her long lashes extended fully ...

They floated to life and detached themselves,
From Angela's tired, troubled eye lids,
They took to the breeze and flapped in the air,
In a sight made to startle cruel kids.

Off to the nasty young lad's house they lurched,
Flying with frightening intent,
Then slipped through keyholes and into his room,
To begin their vengeful event.

The lashes wrapped themselves around his
    ankles,
Then around his mouth and his wrists,
Then just as the boy began to stir,
They tightened with menacing twists!

As they hoisted him up to the ceiling,
The lad cried a muffled scream!
Were these lashes alive and were they for real?
Or part of a petrifying dream!

Angela's lashes took hold of a pen,
And wrote on the boy's bedroom door,
Five words that burned into his memory ...
"Be a bully no more!"

The next day at school, Angela sensed
A change in the lad's disposition,
He looked at her lashes, then cowered away,
Like he'd seen a ghostly apparition.

The boy sat in class, not speaking a word,
Afraid to say "boo to a goose",
For if he didn't change his ways ...
In the next few days ...
Angela's lashes may return as a noose.

Planet Earth

Our planet Earth is quite unique,
You know there's only one,
Why don't we give it more respect?
We're going to miss it when it's gone!
Our planet Earth is really cool,
Don't let it over heat,
Greenhouse gas and global warming,
Are the mistakes we must delete!
Reduce, reuse and recycle,
It will lead to a better planet,
It really isn't all that hard,
It can't be difficult can it?
Let's look at things with a new set of eyes
And cut down on pollution,
Where there's a will, there's always a way,
To find a proper solution!
Oil and gas and nuclear power,
Are things we can't sustain,
There's always the sun, there's always the wind,
The waves and water and rain!
There's even a hot and molten core,
At the centre of our Earth,
Our world has been giving us energy,
Since the moment of its birth.

Environmental responsibility,
Is something we all can take on board,
Cut down the stench of pollution,
With an eco-warrior sword!
So ... we should all look after our planet,
As it looks after me and you,
Without this wonderful world of ours,
What on earth would we all do?

The Alpaca in the Christmas Cracker

I won an Alpaca in a Christmas cracker,
We had to take it to the RSPCA,
But then we had to bring it straight back home
    again,
Because they weren't open on Christmas day.

We sat the Alpaca at our festive table,
So it could join in with our Christmas dinner,
But when it came to using a knife and a fork,
You could tell it was a reluctant beginner.

It struggled to grasp with its hoof like toes,
Its best efforts were all in vain,
Those toes weren't really designed to hold
    cutlery,
More suited to Mexican terrain.

Never the less, we gave it a plate,
As it sat next to our aunt, the librarian,
It turned up its nose to the turkey roast,
As Alpacas are, of course, vegetarian.

It dived in, head first, to a big bowl of spuds,
It devoured a parsnip and sprout,
But we had all neglected to remember one
    thing ...
What goes in ... must also come out.

Poor Aunty Librarian was in such a state!
The whiff was just too much to bear,
So we took the Alpaca out into the garden
And it finished its dinner out there.

Thatcher

A horrible lady called Thatcher,
Was once called the children's milk snatcher,
She did lots of stuff,
That was nasty and rough,
Not even the devil could match her!

John Cena

A strong muscle man called John Cena,
Was thrown out of the wrestling arena,
He was berated,
'Cause he underestimated,
The strength of the town's window cleaner!

Llama

There once was a charming young llama,
Who starred in a TV crime drama,
It studied some clues,
Then announced on the news,
"The culprit is Barack Obama!"

Stephen Fry

A lovely man called Stephen Fry,
Loved to read and travel and fly,
He said "There's nothing finer,
Than a slow boat to China,
Let me give your regards to Shanghai!"

Kamil

There was a cool guy called Kamil,
Who was trained to use a dentist's drill,
He'd inject your gum,
To make it all numb,
Because fixing bad teeth was his skill!

Richards From Limerick

Two men called Richard from Limerick,
Were known as 'big Rick' and 'slimmer Rick'.
One day 'big Rick' swam,
Across to Birmingham,
So now everyone knows him as 'swimmer Rick'.

Barry's Big Brown Magic Conkers

He found them below an old Horse Chestnut
   tree,
Hiding away amidst leafy debris,
Not one, not two, but a marvellous three ...
Barry's big brown magic conkers.

He looked at them shine like magnificent jewels,
As he polished them up with his polishing tools,
They started to spin like enchanting whirlpools ...
Barry's big brown magic conkers.

Barry was drawn into a magical place,
Where a giant conker sat with a smile on its face,
And spoke with warmth and knowledge and
   grace ...
Barry's big brown magic conkers.

It told him of harm some humans were doing,
Pollution and waste and the filth they were
   spewing,
For selfish ends that they were pursuing ...
Barry's big brown magic conkers.

It said to him "Barry, your conkers are ace,
They can do magic all over the place!
Perhaps you can help out the whole human
    race?"
Barry's big brown magic conkers.

Barry's young brain had a buzz of elation,
He could save the whole world from mass
    devastation,
His conkers could bring about real conservation...
Barry's big brown magic conkers.

With a blink of an eye he found himself home,
He recalled the giant conker's wise, dulcet tone,
An eco warrior seed had been sewn!
Barry's big brown magic conkers.

He summoned the conkers' power with a spell,
They took to the sky and one started to swell,
Into a planet sized conker where people could
    dwell!
Barry's big brown magic conkers.

As the world stood and stared at this new
    planet's birth,
Bad humans were sucked from the face of the
    Earth!
And dumped on the conker, for all that it's worth...
Barry's big brown magic conkers.

The conker planet then floated away,
The polluting humans had had their day,
Only the good ones were able to stay ...
Barry's big brown magic conkers.

You could almost hear the Earth's sigh of relief,
No more nastiness, bullying, poison or grief,
Our world was turning over a brand new leaf ...
All because of ...

Barry's big brown magic conkers.

Thank You

This is a list of people who have inspired me, influenced me or helped me in anyway (whether they know it or not). So allow me to say "thank you".

Zack, Fran and Claude xxx
Mama e Papa e la famiglia Esposito
Dreadlockalien
Elvis McGonagall
AF Harrold
John Hegley
John Cooper Clarke
Attila the Stockbroker
Everyone at Birmingham / Worcestershire / Staffordshire / Warwickshire and Shropshire Libraries.
Arts Council (West Midlands)
Apples and Snakes
Polar Bear, Kim, Jodi Anne B, Leon, Loz, Sean, Si, Tim, Charlie, Maggie, Lorna, Abdullah, Amerah, Anisa, Carl, Stringy P, Matt, Kurly, Tony (Longfella), The Anti Poet, Bohdan, Holly McNish, Kate Tempest, Bowie, Lemmy, Tim Minchin, The Ten Letters gang, Skabucks, Vaseline, Sunny and Shay, Northfield Arts Forum, everyone at MAGGS,

everyone at Women & Theatre, The Palace Theatre, Artrix and all my poetry and music friends in and around Brum and the world.

...and anyone else who knows me.

To all the young people and teachers I've met at all the schools I've ever done (and yet to do) poetry workshops at. You are ace.

A Bit About the Author ... Spoz

SPOZ...was born at 44 Kineton Road, Rubery, on the edge of Birmingham in 1964. He became known as 'Spoz' (like his brothers and sister) because it was easier than his real name, 'GIOVANNI ESPOSITO' and happens to be the bit between the 'E' and the 'ito' (sort of).

SPOZ... is an award winning performance poet, singer/songwriter, film maker, playwright, occasional fish re-upholsterer and is the poet-in-residence at Birmingham City FC. He has been seen on BBC and Central Television, has written for, and been heard on BBC Radio Four, Radio Five Live, Radio West Midlands, Radio Coventry & Warwickshire, Capital Gold and on the toilet.

SPOZ... has performed at the Glastonbury festival, Cheltenham Literature festival, Oxford Literature Festival, Warwick Words festival, Ledbury Poetry Festival, Leamington Peace Festival, Bartons Arms Comedy Club, the Shambala festival and in front of his mom.

SPOZ... was 'crowned' Birmingham's eleventh poet laureate in October 2006. He continues to work extensively in schools, lifting the appeal of writing and performing poetry to hitherto, unseen heights.

SPOZ… remains modest and still lives in Birmingham.

SPOZ… has another poetry book available called "The Day the Earth Grew Hair … and other stuff".

SPOZ… has a website. www.spoz.co

SPOZ… looks a bit like Joe Pasquale.